Dear Parents and Educators,

Welcome to Penguin Young Readers! As parents and educators, you know that each child develops at his or her own pace—in terms of speech, critical thinking, and, of course, reading. Penguin Young Readers recognizes this fact. As a result, each Penguin Young Readers book is assigned a traditional easy-to-read level (1–4) as well as a Guided Reading Level (A–P). Both of these systems will help you choose the right book for your child. Please refer to the back of each book for specific leveling information. Penguin Young Readers features esteemed authors and illustrators, stories about favorite characters, fascinating nonfiction, and more!

Pig and Pug

LEVEL 2

GUIDED READING LEVEL **F**

This book is perfect for a **Progressing Reader** who:
- can figure out unknown words by using picture and context clues;
- can recognize beginning, middle, and ending sounds;
- can make and confirm predictions about what will happen in the text; and
- can distinguish between fiction and nonfiction.

Here are some **activities** you can do during and after reading this book:
- Venn Diagram: Pig and Pug are two animals on a farm. Think about how the two are alike and how they are different. Then, on a separate piece of paper, draw a Venn diagram—two circles that overlap. Label one circle "Pig" and the other circle "Pug." Write the traits that are specific to each animal in the parts of the circles that don't touch. Write the traits they share in the space where the circles overlap.
- Creative Writing: This is a story about how an unlikely friendship develops between Pig and Pug. Think of two other animals that are different from each other. It could be a monkey and a horse, a dolphin and a pelican, or any two animals you choose. Write a story about how the two become friends despite their differences.

Remember, sharing the love of reading with a child is the best gift you can give!

—Bonnie Bader, EdM
  Penguin Young Readers program

*Penguin Young Readers are leveled by independent reviewers applying the standards developed by Irene Fountas and Gay Su Pinnell in *Matching Books to Readers: Using Leveled Books in Guided Reading*, Heinemann, 1999.

For Chutley, the pug who changed
our lives forever—LM & ZAM

For my Granny Dot and Grandad Ro—J

PENGUIN YOUNG READERS
Published by the Penguin Group
Penguin Group (USA) LLC, 375 Hudson Street, New York, New York 10014, USA

USA | Canada | UK | Ireland | Australia | New Zealand | India | South Africa | China

penguin.com
A Penguin Random House Company

Text copyright © 2015 by Laura Marchesani. Illustrations copyright © 2015 by Jarvis. All rights reserved.
Published by Penguin Young Readers, an imprint of Penguin Group (USA) LLC, 345 Hudson Street,
New York, New York 10014. Manufactured in China.

Library of Congress Cataloging-in-Publication Data is available.

ISBN 978-0-448-48342-9 (pbk)   10 9 8 7 6 5 4 3 2 1
ISBN 978-0-448-48343-6 (hc)   10 9 8 7 6 5 4 3 2 1

PENGUIN YOUNG READERS

LEVEL
PROGRESSING
READER
2

PIG AND PUG

by Laura Marchesani and Zenaides A. Medina Jr.
illustrated by Jarvis

Penguin Young Readers
An Imprint of Penguin Group (USA) LLC

Pig lives on a farm.

There are four cows.

There are ten chickens.

There are six sheep.

But there is just one pig.

Every morning,

the animals go to work.

The cows give milk.

The chickens lay eggs.

The sheep eat grass.

Pig sleeps alone in his pen.

Every afternoon,

the animals play together.

The cows moo together.

The chickens cluck together.

The sheep baa together.

Pig snorts alone.

Pig wants a friend.

One day, someone new comes to
the farm.

It is not a cow.

It is not a chicken.

It is not a sheep.

Is it a pig?

The cows think it is a pig.

It has a curly tail like a pig.

But it is not a pig.

The chickens think it is a pig.

It snorts like a pig.

But it is not a pig.

The sheep think it is a pig.

It rolls like a pig.

But it is not a pig.

Pig thinks it is a pig.

But it is not a pig.

This is Pug.

Pig and Pug cannot be friends.

But Pug likes to play.

And Pig likes to play.

Pug likes to roll in the mud.

Pig likes to roll in the mud.

Pug likes to eat and eat and eat.

Pig likes to eat and eat and eat.

Pug likes to nap.

Pig likes to nap.

Pig and Pug can be friends!

On the farm, the cows moo and
give milk.

The chickens cluck and lay eggs.

The sheep baa and eat grass.

MILK

And Pig is not alone.